# A Mighty Forest
# A Mighty World

# A Mighty Forest
# A Mighty World

An allegorical review of
where we've been,
where we are,
and where we're called to go

gn holt

Grateful Steps
Asheville, North Carolina

Grateful Steps
Crest Mountain
30 Ben Lippen School Road, Suite 107
Asheville, North Carolina 28806

Library of Congress Number 2017919012
holt, gn
*A Mighty Forest, A Mighty World*
*An allegorical review of*
*where we've been,*
*where we are,*
*and where we're called to go*

ISBN 978-1-935130-19-2  Paperback
Illustration on page 37 by Darcy Whitten

Printed in the USA at
Lightning Source

FIRST EDITION

www.gratefulsteps.org

A long time ago, on a land not so far away, there existed a wonderfully rich and ancient forest. It was one of the most beautiful and bountiful forests ever known. There were lots of songbirds who flitted about the branches, red-headed woodpeckers who hollowed out holes for homes in the tree trunks, and great feathered eagles who soared high in the open sky.

And this forest was so rich with food—fruit was hanging from the tree limbs, acorns were dropping on the ground, worms were wiggling in the soil—that everyone who lived there never had to worry about what they would eat. And these birds were so beautifully adorned with feathers that they never had to worry about what they would wear. And the trees were so diverse in kind and shape and foliage that the birds never had to worry about where or with what they'd build nests in which to rest.

By day they glided to and fro collecting food, alighting on branches to sing their songs, and sailing high above the tree tops. By night they rested securely together in nests of twigs beneath an open and starry sky. And always, always, a wishful and whispering breeze caressed their plumage to remind them of their loving and lofty place within the forest.

It was truly a beautiful place.

Then one day a strange thing happened. From across the great desert appeared a totally new kind of bird. He was a kind of bird that no one in the forest had ever seen before. His feathers were missing, and he couldn't fly. His legs and wings, however, seemed well developed for walking and work.

And when this new bird saw this "new" forest, he was utterly amazed. Here, for him, was a fresh and expansive land where he could have a new beginning —a land of such profound scale and beauty that it was more than he could behold alone.

And so he got very excited to go back to his troubled homeland to tell all of his friends about this discovery.

At first it was one-by-one, then two-by-two, then even ten-by-ten as these new birds began to show up in the forest.

And they, too, were amazed . . . and in awe.

Setting out on their strong and steady legs and utilizing exotic tools and knowledge they had brought with them from across the desert, these new birds worked long and hard to secure a place for themselves on the forest floor.

But it was a strange thing with these new birds. They were so driven and so successful at harvesting their food that some of them had much idle time. And for some reason, idle time was unsettling for them. They really didn't know what to do with it. They didn't know how to enjoy each other's company or the company of the other animals around them. They didn't know how to truly behold the glorious nature and beauty of the forest surrounding them.

And yet they longed for something. They longed for a sense of freedom.

So with the bounty of their harvest and the abundance of their time, these new birds set out to explore ways they might gain that sense of freedom.

One day a couple of the new birds invented a device they called an "auto-hawk." Now an auto-hawk was a strange tube with wings that *looked* like a hawk, but it was fashioned out of a cold, lifeless material. Furthermore, it had no feathers, its wings didn't move, and it couldn't fly on its own. If a bird folded himself up and climbed inside, however, he could control its surfaces and actually lift from the ground and fly through the air!

Now these birds had a taste of the freedom they longed for, and they were happy.

But because these auto-hawks took a lot of time and forest materials to build, more and more new birds were brought over to supply the necessary work and to harvest those materials. And as more and more of these auto-hawks were built, more and more of the new birds harvested more and more worms so that they might trade them for their own auto-hawk. And as more and more of the new birds took to the skies in their own auto-hawks, the airspace in the forest became busier and busier until, eventually, the birds decided room had to be cleared in the forest to make accommodation.

And so they began to chop all the branches off the trees and clear paths on the ground on which to make "landing pads."

Now more new birds than ever had a taste of the freedom they longed for, and they were happy.

Time went on. Days and weeks turned to months and years. The new birds had children, their children had children, and even their children's children had children. The birds of each generation taught their offspring how to build and fly the latest and greatest new auto-hawks so that they too could taste that freedom—*and* get to their share of the harvest.

You see, the auto-hawk was not just for fun and freedom at this point. The new birds now relied on the auto-hawk's range and speed in order to harvest enough worms so that they might eat, *and* enough *extra* worms so that they might trade them for the newest and fastest auto-hawks with all the latest gear.

Eventually the day came when nearly everyone had forgotten about the feathered birds and the original glory of the forest. "Never mind," the new birds said to the few of their children who wondered aloud about those days. "That forest doesn't exist anymore, and flying under your own two wings is way too slow and dangerous, if not impossible altogether. Better to have a lightning-fast auto-hawk."

But as you might have guessed, the time also came when the forest was *so* loud and *so* busy and *so* fast, that many of the younger birds began to wonder if the pursuit of happiness by way of auto-hawk was really the way to go.

They began to search the memories hidden deeply within their brains. They listened to the stories of the few remaining feathered birds about the old days when there were no auto-hawks—the days when everyone was happy flying under their own two wings.

And for this *they* longed.

Some of them longed so much, in fact, that they parked their auto-hawks and climbed up into the trees. And here, for the first time for as long as they could remember, they felt a soft and whispering breeze caressing their skin.

And this, somehow, they recognized.

Could they really believe what it was telling them? Was this breeze *still* alive? *Still* willing and wanting to support feathered birds in natural flight?

Some believed that it was and spent a long time quietly listening to that breeze and getting to know its ways.

Then, after a while, almost without them even noticing, feathers began to grow on the bare skin of these quiet birds. And as more and more feathers grew on their skin, they came to understand and love the breeze more and more. And as they understood the breeze more and more, they were subtly led to the day when some decided it was time to trust . . .

and step forth from their perches . . .

and *fly!*

It . . . was . . . magical

. . . for a moment.

You see, the forest was a very different place by now. These fledgling feathered birds had challenges to face that the feathered birds of the old days didn't have. They had to learn, for instance, that they really couldn't carry much gear when flying under their own two wings. In fact, many learned this the hard way. And many had a hard time putting down all their gear, because gear had become pretty well attached to them.

Furthermore, there was the danger of all that auto-hawk traffic. In fact, some of those trying to fly under their own two wings would do okay for a little while only to get run down by some fast-moving auto-hawk and get their wings broken—or worse.

It was very sad.

Still time went on. The forest grew weaker . . . and darker . . . and less healthy for having all its branches cut off. In addition, the trees really couldn't breathe properly anymore for all the foul air being put out from the backsides of the auto-hawks.

Yet ironically, even with the forest's bounty declining this way, most of the new birds simply continued to build faster and more tightly sealed auto-hawks. This allowed them to get to the few remaining worms in time without having to breathe all that foul air themselves.

At this point, as you might have imagined, many of the feathered birds who wanted to fly under their own two wings—both young and old alike—began to get angry at the new birds flying their auto-hawks.

They began to wonder if they needed to fight.

From all corners of the forest, feathered birds rose up to stake their natural claim to the skies. And from all corners of the world, new birds rose up to claim *their* right to the skies. It was bird against bird—brother against sister, daughter against father, and neighbor against neighbor.

The fighting soon got so bad that more birds were getting hurt—and getting hurt worse—by the fighting than by the competition for the airspace and the worms.

It was really sad.

In fact, it was a mess.

And just when it looked as though the whole forest and all the birds within it would be destroyed . . . someone came.

It was a someone that nearly *everyone* had forgotten.

It was the someone who had planted all the trees of the forest long, long ago—even before *this* story began.

It was . . .

the forest ranger.

And when he beheld the forest and its state, and all the birds and how they were carrying on, he yelled out, "My gracious flock . . ."

"**STOP!**"

"STOP."

"Stop."

Many words of many tones welled up powerfully within him, but before any found their way forth, the sheer scale of the matter rendered him confounded and speechless.

He took a few breaths . . .

Then, finally, with little left but helpless love and unadorned truth, he went on:

"What have you *done?*" he asked.

"What are you *doing?*" he begged.

"Don't you remember this is the forest I have given you . . . to live in, to care for, *to share with each other?*"

"Feathered birds, I know you have every right to be angry. I know you have been hurt . . . and some of you, killed. I know you have been brushed aside, designated 'ill' and locked up in 'zoos' for your struggles with natural potential. I *know* the new birds have all but destroyed this forest and the fresh airspace within it. But those birds *are* your brothers and sisters and fathers and mothers. I know they are strange to you—and blind. But mind your talons, *for those birds are mine as well*—even if they have forgotten. And many of them have indeed given you food and shelter when heavy storms did rage.

"New birds, I know you must eat. I know you have intellectual muscles that are strong and must be flexed, and that your industriousness is unmatched on earth. But I also know there is a space within you so designed that all your auto-hawks or forest materials cannot fill it, *for it is not meant to be filled with those things*. Do not run from what is natural and try to escape it. For under natural truth does the whole forest exist, and it is inescapable. But fear not, for this does not mean there is no room in this forest for you and your ways. In fact, some of your ways have provided even the feathered among you respite when heavy storms did rage.

"Mind your talons. Clean up your ways. Do not oppose me or the feathered birds, for they *do* love you—even if they have forgotten.

"Indeed, have you *all* forgotten,
that by way of my faithful son—that
mighty, gentle dove who lived among
you long, long ago (even before *this*
story began)—and by way of the
love, grace, strength, and sacrifice he
brought forth, you can be reconciled
with what is natural, good, and holy?
I know you miss these things, for there
is that space within you designed to
hold these very things that will give
you life as you have not known it for
so long. I know this space is there, for
it is I who put it there.

"And I *know* you fear you are incapable
of accepting these things, but it is *not*
too late—yet.

"In fact, every day I grieve for my son, who in spirit lies with broken wings and anguished heart upon your forest floor. Every day I call to him saying, 'Enough, child. It is time. You have suffered for so long now. I know you must be starved for clean and living love. I know the life and light within you must be all but extinguished. Please let go, for even I am fearful for you.'

"Yet still he refuses me. 'Not yet, father. Not yet,' he says. 'For there are still so many who are afraid to believe what is at stake. There are still so many who are sinking into the dark depths on account of their attachments and fears. There are still so many of my beloved brothers and sisters who have done so well by me but still deny themselves the life and glory we wish to give.

"'Speak to them, father,' he says. '*Make* them hear the desperation of our hearts and these times. Speak to them, father, for we *cannot* accept their loss, and I cannot hang on much longer.'

"You see, new birds, feathered birds," the ranger went on, "this is how I came to be here now. You are *all* my flock, and I am your *one* father from whom everything that is has come, including each of you. And if, therefore, I am your one father, then how can your differences be irreconcilable? For I am reconciled within myself. Indeed, it is by such reconciliation that so much is born.

"Seek my faithful one and find him. For he is the reconciled son of you and son of me. And oh how he loves his parents, to the point that he has already dedicated and sacrificed his life for the sake of *our* reconciliation. But he *is* still alive, and his spirit is still alive within many of you. *Seek him . . . and find him . . . and follow him.*

"Oh new birds, feathered birds—my troubled children! My dear, sweet flock. How I do love you. But you must know it is not for your stale and stubborn pride. Rather it is for your willingness to behold—even painful truth. It is for your willingness to turn—your willingness to lay your hearts and minds and muscle to the task and forge ahead, even in spite of the odds.

"My dear, sweet flock. Reconcile yourselves with me, and reconciliation with each other will come. For there is such need of you in this universe. There is such a special place for you in the greater kingdom. *There is still so much more . . .*"

And when all the birds heard this,
they did stop.

And they beheld.

And they cried with pain . . . and regret . . . and shame. Yet they also cried with sweet, sweet sorrow for being reminded of their holy, natural roots. And the complexity of their tears was almost more than they could bear, but that mighty dove was there to help them bear it, *and it was good.*

For in their tears and by his grace, the dark marks of their wayward ways were washed clean. And they rediscovered that in the heart of each was a bit of the other. And the ranger's son loved them. And he forgave them. And tears were in his eyes because his brothers and sisters were back.

And he had missed them.

So much.

And after this fresh air—this fresh love and life—had been drawn back into the lungs of all the birds, the forest regained its hope, and the world regained its hope. And with time and a renewed longing for a renewed kind of life—with a renewed sense of mutual place and mutual purpose—the birds came to live together beneath the sun as one, and the ranger's dove himself lived among them.

And in this way, believe it or not,
there will be wholeness,
and there will be freedom,

and life may come to be better
than even it was before . . .

www.ingramcontent.com/pod-product-compliance
Lightning Source LLC
Chambersburg PA
CBHW030553130626
46552CB00006B/2530